WALT DISNEY'S
Lucky Puppy

Adapted from the Walt Disney motion picture "One Hundred and One Dalmatians." Based on the book "The Hundred and One Dalmatians" by Dodie Smith, published by The Viking Press.

TOLD BY JANE WERNER WATSON

PICTURES BY
ALLEN HUBBARD AND DON BESTOR

GOLDEN PRESS   **NEW YORK**

THIS IS A BRAND-NEW BOOK, WRITTEN AND ILLUSTRATED ESPECIALLY FOR GOLDEN BOOKS
THIS LITTLE GOLDEN BOOK WAS PREPARED UNDER THE SUPERVISION OF
THE WALT DISNEY STUDIO

Lucky Puppy lived with his father, Pongo,
and his mother, Perdita,
and with all his sisters and brothers.
The people who belonged to them were
Roger and Anita and Nanny Cook.
(That's Nanny Cook in the doorway above.)

Here are Penny and Lenny
and Salter and Pepper,
Jolly and Rolly and Patch and Latch.

Here are Spot and Dot and Blob and Blot and Blackie and Whitey and— where's Lucky?

Here is Lucky,
in front of the television,
watching his favorite, Thunderbolt.

Whenever Penny and Lenny
wanted to dig holes

or Salter and Pepper
wanted to chew bones

or Patch and Latch
wanted to chase tails

or Jolly and Rolly
wanted to jump at Nanny Cook's apron strings,

or Spot and Dot wanted to play hide and seek

or Blob and Blot wanted to growl at the mirror,

or Blackie and Whitey wanted to take a nap,

Lucky never wanted to.
He just wanted to sit
in front of the television
watching his favorite, Thunderbolt.

Or he practiced television tricks.
"I'm going to be a television star
myself," said Lucky Pup.

Well, all the other puppies learned puppy tricks. Soon they could sit up and roll over.

They could dance
and shake hands.

They could jump for a treat
and walk politely at heel.

But not Lucky.
He was too busy dreaming
of being a television star.

One day he decided he was ready
to be in a television show.
So he slipped out of the house
and he ran down the street.

He ran around a corner.
And there he stopped.
He was lost.
He did not know his way
to the television place.
And he did not know
his way home.

Poor Lucky.
He walked and walked and walked.
He tried to show people
his television tricks.
But they did not understand.
"He doesn't seem to know
any puppy tricks,"
was all the people said.

Finally a policeman came along.
He looked at Lucky's license tag.
And he took Lucky home.

There were Penny and Lenny
and Salter and Pepper
and Jolly and Rolly
and Patch and Latch,

Spot and Dot and Blob and Blot
and Blackie and Whitey,
all doing puppy tricks for treats.
But not Lucky.

Lucky was all tired out.
He crept straight into his basket.
And he went straight to sleep.

He even slept through
the Thunderbolt Show
which the other puppies watched.

But next morning
Lucky was up first of all.
"Time enough for television later," he said.
"Now I am going to learn my puppy tricks."
And he did!